Barbie

A Happy Holiday

This story and artwork have been adapted from Barbie: Holiday Helpers.

By Diane Muldrow

Cover photography: Willy Lew, Laura Lynch, Greg Roccia, Teri Weber, Judy Tsuno, and Lisa Collins
Interior photography: Paul Chamberlain, Laura Lynch, Lars Auvinen, Patrick Kittel,
Barb Miller, Henrique Bagulho, and Lisa Collins

A GOLDEN BOOK • NEW YORK
Golden Books Publishing Company, Inc., New York, New York 10106

Barbie was having fun cross-country skiing when suddenly a gust of wind blew her hat off her head. Barbie skied through the woods after it.

Her hat finally landed outside a quaint
cottage, where a man said, "Good morning,
young lady. Are you lost?"

"Good morning to you, too, sir,"
Barbie replied. "Actually my hat was
lost, but I've just found it."

The man invited Barbie inside his workshop.

"My name is Peter Flanders," he said. "Would you like some hot tea?"

"I'm Barbie. Tea would be nice," said Barbie as she stepped out of her skis.

Barbie took a look around the workshop.
"What beautiful toys!" she exclaimed.

"Every year I make toys for the underprivileged children in town," said Mr. Flanders. "But I might not get the toys to the kids in time for the holidays this year. My car won't start."

"Don't worry, Mr. Flanders," said Barbie. "I'd be glad to drive you into town."

Mr. Flanders smiled. "How can I ever thank you?" he asked.

"You could let me interview you," Barbie replied. "I'm a reporter for the Evening News. You and your toys would make a great story!"

Barbie called Jan, her story editor. Jan worked at the news station.

"Hello, Jan," said Barbie. "I just came across a terrific story about a nice man who makes wonderful toys. Do you like the idea?. . . Great, we'll meet you and the TV crew at the City Children's Home in two hours."

Barbie finished her tea and stepped back into her skis. Then she rushed home to get a change of clothes.

Mr. Flanders had the toys ready to go
by the time Barbie returned.

At the children's home, Barbie introduced
Mr. Flanders to the news crew. Then Katie,
the sound engineer, attached a microphone
to Mr. Flanders's sweater.

Just then, a group of children rushed
in to give Mr. Flanders a hug. They
remembered him from last year.

As Barbie changed her clothes, the
cameraman filmed Mr. Flanders and
the children.

Barbie began the interview by looking into the camera. "I'm at the City Children's Home with Mr. Peter Flanders," announced Barbie. "Every year he makes toys and gives them to children as holiday presents."

Barbie turned to Mr. Flanders and asked, "What do you like best about making toys?"

"I love to see children smile!" replied Mr. Flanders as he handed a toy train to a happy little boy.

After all the children had received their toys, the crew decided to film Mr. Flanders at work. The interview was almost over.

"Thanks to Mr. Flanders, many children will enjoy a very special holiday," Barbie said to the camera. "For the Evening News, I'm Barbie, wishing you happy holidays!"